VALENTINE'S LITTLE

An ABDL MMM Story

Michael Levi

INTRODUCTION

"It's Valentine's Day, the same when you found me at that party."

"Ah, of course. I was only testing you to make sure that you remember it," he said, pulling the gluey straps and then taking off my diaper. He did it so easily that I almost didn't feel the material sliding off.

"It smells pretty bad," he added before tossing the diaper into the diaper genie. The changing table that I was lying on was pretty big and it didn't wobble, even though I wasn't that skinny anymore.

Still skinny, but I'd been gaining some pounds since our first meeting.

He reached out below it with his hand and then grabbed a bottle with some deliciously smelling powder inside it and another bottle with cream for my sensitive skin. They were of the highest-quality brands, which was only one more thing about him that proved the strength of his love for me.

He applied the cream and the powder after using some wipes to clean me up.

"You didn't poop, so you don't need a bath, thank goodness," he said, his voice soothing and calming...

CONTENTS

CHAPTER 1

It was Valentine's Day night, and I didn't know what I was going to wear for the party. My friends told me to come as my normal self, but they didn't know me. They all thought I was like them. Just another guy trying to make it in life and meet his boyfriend.

Except that I could never be like them.

I didn't fit in. I was their friend only because I didn't want to feel alone and forgotten. While growing up and even now I had a pretty serious case of incontinence. It happened so often that I couldn't go out without a diaper or a pull-up on.

Over time, I was forced to choose different kinds of diapers so that I didn't feel like an alien. They had cartoon stamps, and even the one that I put on for tonight had Mickey Mouse doodles drawn all over it.

I was standing in front of the door to the fraternity party. The whole building was shaking like it had gained life. My friends had gone in without me and were partying, dancing, and singing. The music that they were playing was a curious mix of hip-hop and dubstep.

I didn't like it, but as soon as a man opened the door for me, I got a boner everywhere I looked. It was like this fraternity house had been built for me and this Valentine party.

I couldn't believe there could ever be so many hot men per square foot.

But they were all not looking at me at all.

They were all throwing their bodies around, kissing, and sometimes even fucking other guests. I felt like I was a fish in a pretty big pond with no limits, as if it was infinite.

And yet I soon noticed that something odd was at play here. There was a man – or more like a guy that looked like a cop standing on the other side of the living room, his eyes looking at me as if he knew that I wasn't who I was trying to look to other people.

There was no malice in his eyes. They looked at me with a layer of understanding and calmness that pulled me to him. I soon found myself padding to him, dodging the other guests while they still partied as if this was the end of the world and not just another day in it.

He sat down at the only table that stood near him, pulling a chair for me and pouring some red wine in a small glass for me. He didn't say anything. Our mutual understanding seemed to be entering levels I never thought possible.

He poured some wine for himself as well. I couldn't help but admire his looks. He looked everything one could ever want in a Daddy.

Finding one was all sorts of difficult. I didn't think I had any chance in that field.

His eyes were ocean-blue, short blond hair, and his skin was peachy-white. The number of wrinkles on his face betrayed his real age, though. He wasn't another student like everyone else in here.

Oh no, he was most likely a professor out here looking for easy prey like me.

He took a sip from his wine glass, putting it down and then telling me a little bit about himself. I was right. He was a professor. History professor, focusing on the Victorian era. His voice was so soothing, so inviting that I kept listening to it for what appeared to have been hours.

He was doing all of this to reel me in to him, and I couldn't help but not even try to fight my temptations.

It didn't take him long to say that he'd been looking for someone like me. He was a Mister seeking his little and through some search – or more like stalking, but at the moment that seemed pretty irrelevant – he found that I was one.

His hand grabbed mine as he took me from the frat house to his mansion overlooking the city. When he parked his car in his garage and I was allowed to admire the city, he showed me what he'd been hiding in his mansion.

My eyes spotted many maids and other workers living in it, but I was pretty sure that they kept their lips sealed about the kind of things that he liked to do when nobody was looking.

And he didn't just have some toys for littles like myself, but rather a whole room where I fit in like a glove. I couldn't even remember the party that I was supposed to be enjoying with my friends.

They weren't really my friends, though. More like they always made everything about themselves and remembered me only when they needed good grades on some assignments.

Anyway, enough about them.

My eyes were gleaming with happiness while I took in the room where I was in. I was happy beyond measure, with the first thing I did as soon as he allowed me in here being something that I'd been thinking about since getting to that frat house.

I took off all of my clothes, keeping only the diaper on. I looked like a proper little now. My hand was holding a binky and I was ready to crawl around in his estate for hours on end until he came to play with me as well.

My life here was going to be so different and excellent, and the good thing was that I didn't have to tell anyone about it.

I didn't owe any explanation to anybody, and for the time being, I was going to keep studying and attending classes. The last thing I wanted was someone hurrying over to the police to assemble a search party for me.

I wasn't going to allow that to happen.

CHAPTER 2

Mister Roder was his name. It's how he liked to call himself anyway. And he wasn't just handsome, but he was also pretty big for a guy. He was so big that he made me feel smaller than usual, and that was quite the accomplishment.

I was already pretty skinny and small for a man. I'd always been this way and I didn't think it was ever going to change.

It was a different morning when I woke up. A different day, but already one year since I met him. Ever since then, he hadn't done anything special with me. I was still a virgin through and through.

While I was going to college and he always took me to classes, he took care of everything I needed. This morning wasn't going to be much different.

He allowed me to sleep without an onesie tonight. There was a website that sold clothes like those for littles like myself, and Mister always bought a whole collection of them for me. The closet was always full.

I grabbed my binky, slid it into my mouth, and started to suck on it. The teat part of it always made me feel as if everything was going to be okay, no matter what came to pass.

I was lying in the adult-sized crib that he already had prior to my coming here. He always put me inside it every night, and last night was no different. I could still feel his hands grabbing me. He was so strong that he could do it so easily, always with a big and comforting smile on his face.

I sat up in the crib and gripped the railing. It was past the time that he was supposed to come here to check up on me. I wasn't worried that something bad happened to him, though. Mister was the kind of man that could challenge the whole world and win.

I was suckling on my paci when my hand found my teddy sitting on the other side of the crib. As soon as my eyes landed on him, I snagged him and hugged him. His fur felt so comforting against my skin.

But then a smell floating in the air caught my attention. It was my diaper. I'd messed it tonight. I couldn't believe it! I thought that I'd been making some progress in the incontinence department, but it seemed that wasn't the case.

The smell was quite bad, making me wish that my Mister was right here in my room, getting his hands ready to change my dirty diaper. I didn't poop in it, though.

I was about to fuss when the door swung open, Mister stepping through it with a big smile on his face. He didn't wear clothes. He wore just a pair of light blue boxers, his bulge already stealing the attention of my eyes.

I couldn't look at anything else while he strolled as if he didn't just own this massive estate, but also the whole city.

"Look who's messed his diaper," he said, lowering the railing of his crib and picking me up in his arms.

He carried me from the crib to the changing table, one of his hands taking the paci out of my mouth.

"You can talk now if you want."

"Are you going to buy something for me today?"

"Why? What's so special about today?"

"It's Valentine's Day, the same when you found me at that party."

"Ah, of course. I was only testing you to make sure that you remember it," he said, pulling the gluey straps and then taking off my diaper. He did it so easily that I almost didn't feel the material sliding off.

"It smells pretty bad," he added before tossing the diaper into the diaper genie. The changing table that I was lying on was pretty big and it didn't wobble, even though I wasn't that skinny anymore.

Still skinny, but I'd been gaining some pounds since our first meeting.

He reached out below it with his hand and then grabbed a bottle with some deliciously smelling powder inside it and another bottle with cream for my sensitive skin. They were of the highest-quality brands, which was only one more thing about him that proved the strength of his love for me.

He applied the cream and the powder after using some wipes to clean me up.

"You didn't poop, so you don't need a bath, thank goodness," he said, his voice soothing and calming.

He reached below the changing table and grabbed a brand-new diaper, which he took no time to put on me. He connected the straps gently with his fingers before patting the front.

"So, what do you think? Feeling like a different person now?"

"Yes, Mister!"

His hand caressed my cheek.

"You're so cute it's unbelievable. And yeah, don't worry about the anniversary of our first meeting. I do have something for you, though you're going to have to play a little game with me first to find out what it is."

"Oh, really? I'm happy that you have planned something for today. I almost thought that you were going to forget about it, with you being so busy all the time."

Mister was pretty busy, but that didn't mean that he didn't spend enough time with me. Actually, he made me feel pretty spoiled. He bought me so many things and spent so much time with me that it was unbelievable that he still had a life outside of his estate.

"Yes, and at the end of our little game, you're going to be wishing that it was Valentine's Day every day."

"Now you're making me blush," he said, taking me to his bedroom, where we could have all the privacy we needed.

The walls were sound-proof, so whatever happened here, nobody was going to hear it.

Nobody but the hulking men that he'd invited to come to meet me.

CHAPTER 3

It was a Valentine's Day decorated bedroom, with heart-shaped neon signs hanging from the walls, a big heart-shaped light bulb that hung from the ceiling, and small tables with rose bouquets on top of them.

There were also some heart-shaped cookie cutter wind chimes, painted mason jar lanterns, and the walls had been painted with a soft tone of red.

Everything was red, which contrasted with the colors of the underwear of the men that now surrounded me.

There were three of them, including Mister himself.

His little game with me was going to involve something naughty and filthy. He'd planned for this for a very long time, and now he was going to reap the benefits.

"So, this is the little one, huh?" One of his friends asked before sweeping me up in his arms and taking me to the heart-shaped double bed. I almost felt like I was in some kind of motel.

His nose was soon sniffing my skin, going as far as stopping when he reached my diaper.

"Not going to take it off now, of course. That's something I'm going to leave for your Mister."

Mister soon took his place, but his hands didn't go for the straps of my diaper. No, they were groping me, loving me, and his lips were kissing me, too. Lying on this super-soft mattress, I felt exposed and safe at the same time.

I knew that they were only going to do what I wanted.

And what other game could this have been anyway?

It was always going to be this one, where they all took me as they wished.

I couldn't hope to stop Mister, his hands already enough to make it impossible for me to breathe. Every time I breathed, it felt so difficult. I felt my skin getting hotter and hotter, and underneath my diaper, my dick was wild.

It couldn't be compared to theirs, of course. Theirs were much bigger, meatier, thicker, and with so many more bulging veins.

And that's without mentioning that they all knew how to use it. I was nothing more than their plaything now, and soon they were going to make me their cum dump, too.

I couldn't wait for that to happen.

Mister stepped aside and allowed someone else to grace me with his fingers. He knew how to hit all the right spots without making me giggle. My shaft was so hard it was pulsing and making me wonder if I wasn't going to orgasm multiple times.

I was moaning when the next big dude replaced him, his mouth nearing my ear as he spoke, "Tonight, you're never going to forget this."

And I knew that he spoke the truth.

The longer this went on, the more details of it I was going to remember for the rest of my life.

It took no time for Mister to take off my diaper. It only lasted some minutes with me, but that was okay. He could put another on me soon, or he could still use the same one. It didn't matter, as long as I was diapered.

"Ohhh, look at this pretty little thing," one of the guys said, wrapping his fingers around the base of my cock.

He only needed to use three of them, making me feel even smaller than usual.

I dared to open my eyes, only to find him and his chiseled face standing right in front of me. His smile was naughty as something came across his mind. He wasn't going to ask for my permission.

His hand began to pump my little pee-pee. The pace was slow and excruciating at first, just acclimatizing me to the grip of his hand. He knew what he was doing. How many times in his life did he give a man a handjob?

When he picked up his pace, it didn't take me too long to cum. I was shooting my jizz all over myself, my body convulsing. All the guys standing in the room then scooted over to me, leaning down as they put their tongues out.

They licked my belly and legs clean. I hadn't cummed in quite a while. When I finally did it again, it felt like it was never going to end. I couldn't even breathe properly right now. The intensity of my orgasm was almost a bit too much for me.

Mister pushed the other two to the side, kissing me with his cum-coated lips. I was tasting the smell of my own sperm, and it felt wonderful. Still not as good as the flavor of his lips, though.

His hands groped me for what appeared to have been an eternity before he finally flipped me around in the bed, making me bend my body with my butt aimed at the ceiling.

Their hands made love with it, parting my buttcheeks until my orifice was ready for their invasion.

And yet, I didn't think that it was quite going to happen now. I thought that they were going to wait, to ready it for the incredible ramming of me. And I knew that they were not going to be gentle.

Their lips peppered my butt with impossible kisses that made me moan. I couldn't believe that they were still taking so much time to get to the most awaited part of this, with them ramming me with all their might.

I wanted to lose my virginity so bad, and they just kept tempting me instead of doing it.

These men were merciless.

CHAPTER 4

But it turned out that they were just waiting for the right moment to do it. One of their dicks prodded the entrance of my orifice after he climbed up on the bed. The mattress sunk under his weight.

When I was going to turn my head to look at him, he put a blindfold on me.

"You're not allowed to see what might hurt you, little one."

They all chuckled, his dick forcing its way in. I couldn't feel anything other than his girth penetrating me as if I was nothing. I moaned as pain shot through my body, claiming every part of it, but I didn't try to tell him that he was hurting me.

I knew that he was doing this for my own benefit, even if the pain was a part of it, too.

It took him no time to pick up his pace, after he started sliding it in and out of me. His massive slab of meat was more than that – it felt like he'd gotten some kind of implant or something to make it bigger than it first was.

His cock twitched moments before gracing me with his warm seeds. I couldn't help but moan when a climax overtook me, making me convulse underneath the might of his body.

His muscles flexed as he kept ramming me even after that finished, showing me that he was more than willing to come for the second time in a row inside me.

But that didn't mean that the other Misters were okay with that, too.

They could never be.

As soon as he slowed his pace down a little, one of them looped his arms around his torso and yanked him off the bed. They fell on the floor with a loud thud, the crimson and golden lights of the bedroom still making me feel like I was in some kind of party.

It was Mister Roder that took his place, licking my tight orifice with his tongue.

"Hmmm, it's so delicious," he said, lapping up some of the cum that managed to seep out when the other big guy was yanked out of me.

I wished he was still inside me, stretching my walls to their absolute limits. I felt incomplete without a cock inside me.

And it seemed that Mister Roder knew that as well, for he was soon easing himself inside me. The other guys were still fighting each other. Mister had all the time in the world to have his way with me now.

When he was inside me, I couldn't believe what he was making me feel.

He was actually bigger than the other one.

It took him no time to begin sliding in and out of me, his muscles flexing. I couldn't see anything. I couldn't see his muscles actually contracting and expanding, but I could feel them doing those things.

His balls were in minutes slapping off of my asscheeks. His cock was becoming hotter, and I knew that soon he was going to be adding his milk to that of the other Mister that also had his way with me.

I moaned and groaned, now wishing that they were both inside of me.

His dick was twitching some seconds later inside of me. He squirted out his milk in hot jets soon after, gracing me with their warmth. I felt even more pain this time than before, but it was still not enough to make me feel ready to stop this.

I could never.

I wasn't going to ask them to stop.

Mister pulled out of me with a plucking sound, climbing off the bed as the other Mister, a Latino guy with a huge, menacing dick, took his place.

"Now, it's my time," he teased, shoving his massive prick inside me without first trying to make it feel good or gentle.

I knew that he was a Latino because of his Spanish-accented English.

I didn't think it possible, but his shaft felt even bigger than those of the guys that came before him. He stretched my rectum to its absolute limits, and it seemed that he was going to be rougher than the others.

He wasn't just having his way with me now, he was ending me. After he was done, I didn't think that I was going to manage to come out of this as the same little.

I could hear the bed creaking, his prick too irresistible for me. It wasn't long until he was pumping his load out, and it felt like it was never going to end. It just kept coming out, more and more, making me feel a mountain of bliss.

I plopped down on the bed when he pulled out of me. And despite looking so tired, I knew that they weren't quite done with me yet.

One of them plopped down on the bed too, yanking me to him before forcing his dick into my mouth.

I had no choice but to open it.

I knew that he wanted me to give him a blowjob.

I still had my blindfold on, so I didn't know who was doing what.

I was bobbing up and down on his length for what appeared to be an eternity, the other two guys from before popping up behind me and easing their shafts into my waiting asshole.

I was losing my mouth virginity while they fucked me from behind for the second time. I didn't know what was making me feel more turned on. And at that moment, I cummed for the second time.

It all hit the belly of the Mister that was forcing me to give him head. One of the other guys scooted right over and then lapped up my spunk for the second time.

I couldn't believe how right and wrong that felt.

The Mister whose cock I was worshipping pumped his load out inside my mouth, going as far as shoving his length down my throat, too.

My gag reflexes kicked in, but I didn't allow them to ruin this perfect moment I was sharing with them. A tear broke out and rolled down my cheek, but that was okay.

He shoved me to his side, making me lie on Mister Roder's bed. As they all got dressed and then strolled out of the room, I was left with just one question in my mind.

When were they going to come and do this with me again?

The End

BOOKS BY THIS AUTHOR

Rub My Belly: An Abdl Mm Pet Play Romance

It was an accidental encounter. Mike, who had turned 19 not too long ago, never once thought that he was going to meet a man like Richard. He's imposing, tall, and ticks all the right boxes. And even better, he's also a caretaker and a handler. He can make all of his dreams – sweet and naughty alike – come true.

It's going to happen tonight. Mike is going to dress up, get diapered, and crawl around while playing fetch with his Master. Richard is also not going to miss the chance to rub his lean, smooth belly. His little will be wagging his tail as they prepare for the naughty part of their night. And when it happens, swords will cross.

Rub my Belly is a steamy MM short romance, and all the characters in it are consenting adults roleplaying. If you're looking for a story that mixes sweetness and indecency, then this is going to scratch your itch.

Belly Rubbed: An Abdl Mm Pet Play Romance

Thomas knows that life is stressing Daniel out too much, and he needs to do something about it. As a Handler and a Mister, he specializes in making younger men like his secretary feel loved, naughty, and submissive at the same time. And he's been eyeing up Daniel since when he hired him.

He knows that his impossibly cute secretary can become much more than he is. After finally making a decision, he's going to introduce his employee into the world of age play, and there will be plenty of leashes involved. Thomas can already imagine the kind of filthy and sweet things they are going to do together...

Belly Rubbed is a steamy MM short romance, and all the characters in it are consenting adults roleplaying. If you're looking for a story that mixes sweetness and indecency, then this going to scratch your itch.

Follow My Rules: An Abdl Mm Pet Play Story

Breaking up with his Mister caused his life to spiral out of control. After almost getting kicked out of his favorite nightclub, Alan's eyes lock with those of a man that looks too perfect to be real. Muscles on top of muscles, bulging biceps, and a pair of dominant hands are only the tip of the iceberg. His confident and caring personality can make Alan do anything for him, including becoming his docile little pet.

A collar is set to start the beginning of their filthy relationship. As a little, Alan is totally off-limits, but that won't stop Mister Harry from devouring his tunnel. He'll set the rules and his sunshine will have to follow them to the letter. If he doesn't, punishments will make something in his diaper throb...

Follow my Rules is a steamy MM short romance, and all the characters in it are consenting adults roleplaying. If you're looking for a story that mixes sweetness and indecency, then this going to scratch your itch.

Collared Little: An Abdl Mm Pet Play Story

Arf! Arf!

Kevin is a little through and through, but that doesn't mean it's everything he is. With paws and a tail, he now crawls around with a collar around his neck. He calls his Dom his Master, and they are having the time of their lives before they get caught up in a snowstorm.

Trapped, they don't have much in terms of entertainment, which means playing with things they otherwise wouldn't. A plug is only going to be the beginning, and the collar will define the duration of their stay in the mountains. Can he withstand the round of punishments that he's willingly going to subject himself to? There's only one way to find out…

Dear reader, this is the fourth book of the Tempting Age Gaps series. The books are standalones, but they are best read together. If you are looking for a story with forbidden age gaps, doms, littles, and subs, then you need to look no further.

All characters are consenting adults.

ABOUT THE AUTHOR

Michael Levi is a gay erotica author, although he does have some successful non m/m works in his collection. Knowing for hitting all the sweet spots of the reader and leaving everlasting impressions, his stories are not for those weak of the heart.

His works are perfect for readers looking for alpha males, bad boys, and tales with a touch of intimacy in every kiss. Michael Levi is known not just for telling a story, but also for exciting, engaging and arousing the reader.